*For my mother, who always told me I should write,
and for my father, who always believed I would.
Thank you both for being right, again.*
—S. D.

*To my mother, Eileen Patricia Donovan,
who loves reading books to children and
always adds a dash of her own sparkle*
—K. W.

For Nick, my buddy
—V. T.

Farrar Straus Giroux Books for Young Readers
An imprint of Macmillan Publishing Group, LLC
120 Broadway, New York, NY 10271 • mackids.com

ABOUT THIS BOOK

The illustrations for this book were created digitally.
The book was edited by John Morgan and designed by Carolyn Bull and Elynn Cohen.
The production was supervised by John Nora, and the production editors were Hayley Jozwiak and Ilana Worrell.

Library of Congress Cataloging-in-Publication Data is available.

Our books may be purchased in bulk for promotional, educational, or business use.
Please contact your local bookseller or the Macmillan Corporate and Premium Sales Department
at (800) 221-7945 ext. 5442 or by email at MacmillanSpecialMarkets@macmillan.com.

First edition, 2022
Color separations by Embassy Graphics
Printed in China by RR Donnelley Asia Printing Solutions Ltd.,
Dongguan City, Guangdong Province.

ISBN 978-1-250-77476-7 (hardcover)
1 3 5 7 9 10 8 6 4 2

Should this book you try to mop,
You'll be read until you drop.
Better borrow, buy, or trade,
Lest you catch some nasty shade.

Miss Rita,
Mystery Reader

Sam Donovan & Kristen Wixted
Illustrated by Violet Tobacco

Farrar Straus Giroux
New York

"Good morning, Daddy!"
Tori leaped out of bed.
"Good morning, Pumpkin," said Daddy.
"You're Mystery Reader in my class today!"
said Tori.

Daddy winked.
"Shhh . . . it's supposed
to be a surprise."
"But I get to know the
surprise." Tori giggled.

"That's because you asked me to dress up as Miss Rita," he said. "And you'll help me, right?"

"Right. Because sparkle is . . ."

"Serious business," finished Daddy.

Tori clapped their hands. "You're going to love all my friends!"

"I bet!"

"First, a shave."

"Wait!" said Tori as Daddy raised the shaver to his brow.

"Can Miss Rita not shave off Daddy's eyebrows?"

"I suppose." Daddy put down the shaver.

"Let's get to the fun part. You choose a brush."

"I'll be right back with your wig," said Tori.

Tori had a hard time deciding.
Which wig would their class like best?

Lashes

Lips

Tori picked up the jewelry box. Oh my! Rubies and diamonds and pearls spilled all over the floor. Tori gasped. "Oops."

Miss Rita waved it off. "Don't worry, they're plastic."
She sifted through. "These earrings. This ring." She held
up some beads with a flourish. "And *this* necklace?"
   "No, *this* necklace," decided Tori.

"Thank you," said Miss Rita.
"Because sparkle is . . ."
   "Serious business," Tori finished
with a half smile.

Miss Rita pointed to the closet.
"Will you choose a gown?
I'll scoop these up."

But Tori was nervous they wouldn't
be able to pick the perfect gown.

Glamour

Glimmer

"Glasses! Tori, I'll need my reading glasses,"
said Miss Rita, picking up her bedazzled frames.
"Now I'm ready to read!" She winked.

She asked, "What do
you call a dinosaur with
high heels?"
"What?" said Tori.
"My-feet-are-saurus!"

Usually, this was Tori's favorite joke. But all of a sudden, Tori didn't feel like laughing.

"Is today's sparkle more serious than usual?" asked Miss Rita.

When Tori didn't answer, Miss Rita bent down on one knee. "Is everything okay, Pumpkin?"

Tori whispered, "I just want my friends to love Miss Rita as much as I do."

"Pumpkin," said Daddy. "You know that when I get dressed up as Miss Rita, it's just the same as anyone else getting dressed for work. Lawyers have suits, doctors have lab coats, and I have wigs and beads and glittery capes.

"But if you think it's better for me to dress like the rest of your class, I can just be Daddy today."

Tori said, "I think I have an idea . . ."

Later that morning, Tori's class was sitting quiet and ready.
But where was Tori?

"Friends," said the teacher, "today, our Mystery Reader is . . .

"... MISS RITA BOOK!"

Miss Rita sashayed in to cheers from Tori's class. She bowed. "I hope you're ready," she said. "I promise I know how to *read* a book!"

Miss Rita gestured behind her. "May I introduce my new assistant:

Miss Tori Teller entered the classroom, proudly rolling a glittery suitcase.

"We always say," Miss Rita said, "sparkle is . . ."

"...serious business,"

finished Miss Teller.

They handed out wigs and beads and glittery capes to everyone who wanted them.

And a very sparkly story time began.

Authors' Note

Hi! This is Sam and Kristen, and we wanted to share some of the things we know about drag artists and drag culture! Drag is an art form like painting or theater, and each artist is telling a story or sharing a message with their art.

You might have heard of drag queens, but there are also drag kings, drag kids—and even some drag cats! Some drag artists like to use their makeup and costumes to show that everything isn't what it seems. Other drag artists like to point out how silly it is that some people expect everyone to look or act a certain way based on what gender they were assigned at birth. Some drag artists choose serious names, and others choose funny names, because drag is whatever the drag artist wants it to be. Drag performances often include music, dancing, and lip-synching. And sometimes drag performers read picture books to an audience!

As Daddy explains to Tori, it's his job to dress up in wigs and beads and glittery capes. When he's not working, he doesn't dress up. Daddy's pronouns are he/him/his; Miss Rita's pronouns are she/her/hers.

"Drag performer" isn't the same as "transgender." Drag performers are people who dress up to entertain and inspire. Transgender people do not identify with the gender they were assigned at birth.

Tori is a gender-non-binary child. Tori's pronouns are they/them/theirs. "Gender binary" is a phrase that describes when a person feels secure in thinking of themselves as a boy or a girl (or a man or a woman). A lot of people feel comfortable identifying as one of these two genders. But there are also many people who don't feel like either of those words describes them, and so they are non-binary. It's important to respect how everyone identifies themselves.

Did you notice the names of Tori's cats? Marsha P. and Sylvia are named after two very important people who were part of the fight for LGBTQIA+ rights. Those letters stand for lesbian, gay, bisexual, transgender, queer (or questioning), intersex, and asexual, and the + is for others who don't feel covered by any of the previous terms. People who fight for the rights of the LGBTQIA+ community are known as LGBTQIA+ activists. Straight, cisgender people who support the LGBTQIA+ community are called allies. Back to the cats' names! Marsha P. Johnson was a Black trans woman, and Sylvia Rivera was a Latinx trans woman; both became gay rights activists in the 1960s. Sometimes together, sometimes with other people, Marsha P. and Sylvia worked hard in and around New York City, protesting unfair treatment of the queer community. They also set up housing and programs so LGBTQIA+ youth could be themselves, love who they wanted, and be safe.

As for us—Sam and Kristen—we're related! Sam was on *Project Runway* a couple of times, so he's very good at sewing and making clothes. One time during the taping of *Project Runway All Stars*, he and some other designers snuck out to a drag show featuring Monét X Change. After that, Sam fell in love with drag! So he used his sewing expertise to make costumes for drag queens. For the past several years, he's made every kind of drag costume, from an ice queen gown to a fur bikini. Sam brought Kristen to her first drag show. Before *RuPaul's Drag Race* was on TV, she was writing and raising her three kids in suburban Massachusetts and had the chance to be Mystery Reader in classrooms many times. She never ran into any drag queens at the grocery store or anything, so she didn't know much about them. Since she loves theater and going to shows of all kinds, she found that watching drag queens perform was super fun!